THE STORY OF THE PHOENIX SUNS

HORRY
25
SUNS
7
HOUSTON
30
HARP

THE NBA: A HISTORY OF HOOPS

THE STORY OF THE PHOENIX SUNS

NATE FRISCH

CREATIVE EDUCATION

Published by Creative Education
P.O. Box 227, Mankato, Minnesota 56002
Creative Education is an imprint of The Creative Company
www.thecreativecompany.us

Design and production by Blue Design
Art direction by Rita Marshall
Printed in the United States of America

Photographs by AP Images (ASSOCIATED PRESS), Corbis (Mark Goldman/Icon SMI, Mark Halmas/Icon SMI, Reuters), Getty Images (Andrew D. Bernstein/NBAE, Vernon Biever/NBAE, David Cannon, Hank Delespinasse/Sports Illustrated, James Drake/Sports Illustrated, Stephen Dunn, Barry Gossage/NBAE, Andy Hayt/NBAE, Jed Jacobsohn, John W. McDonough/Sports Illustrated, Fernando Medina/NBAE, Manny Millan/Sports Illustrated, Ronald C. Modra, NBA Photos/NBAE, Dick Raphael/Sports Illustrated, David Sherman/NBAE), Newscom (ANDREW GOMBERT/EPA, Jim Ruymen UPI Photo Service)

Library of Congress Cataloging-in-Publication Data
Frisch, Nate.
The story of the Phoenix Suns / Nate Frisch.
p. cm. — (The NBA: a history of hoops)
Includes index.
Summary: An informative narration of the Phoenix Suns professional basketball team's history from its 1968 founding to today, spotlighting memorable players and reliving dramatic events.
ISBN 978-1-60818-445-3
1. Phoenix Suns (Basketball team)—History—Juvenile literature. I. Title.

GV885.52.P47F76 2014
796.323'640979173—dc23 2013039313

CCSS: RI.5.1, 2, 3, 8; RH.6-8.4, 5, 7

First Edition
9 8 7 6 5 4 3 2 1

Cover: Guard Goran Dragic
Page 2: Guard Kevin Johnson (#7)
Pages 4-5: Guard Jason Richardson, center Louis Amundson
Page 6: Guard Quentin Richardson, forward Shawn Marion

KERS

RICHARDSON
3
FINLEY
4

TABLE OF CONTENTS

COURTSIDE STORIES

INTRODUCING...

BASKETBALL BLOOMS IN THE DESERT

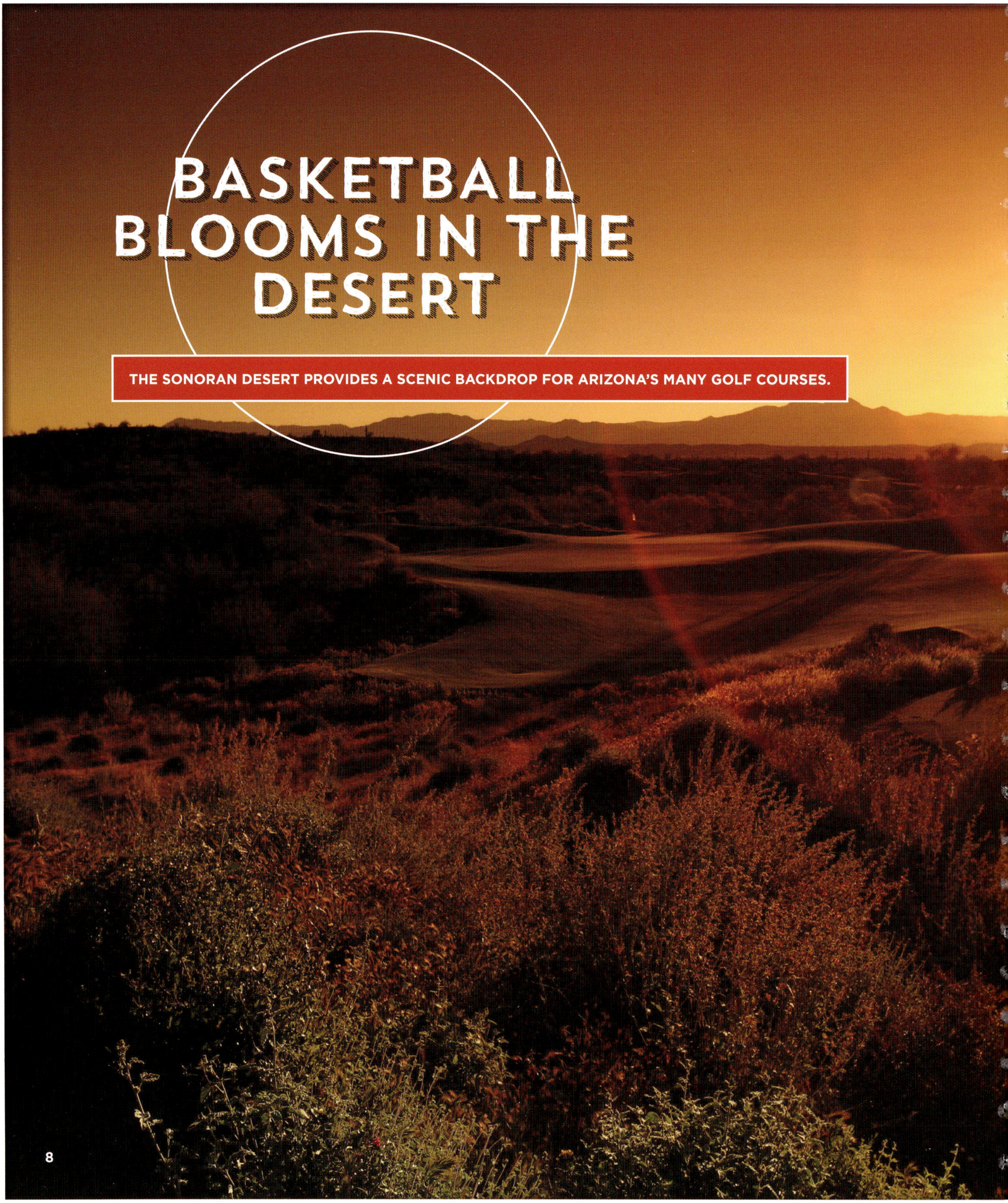

THE SONORAN DESERT PROVIDES A SCENIC BACKDROP FOR ARIZONA'S MANY GOLF COURSES.

PAUL SILAS

“I’m off to Pumpkinville.” Such a declaration may have been made in the 1860s near what is now Phoenix, Arizona. Taking advantage of the irrigation system the native Hohokam people had left behind, settlers experienced success with crops such as pumpkins. Before long, the settlement was renamed “Phoenix,” because the town was reborn from an older city. Today, Phoenix is the capital city of Arizona and headquarters to various companies such as American Express and Best Western hotels. The warm climate of “The Valley of the Sun” also makes it a popular winter destination for tourists.

As its population and tourism increased, Phoenix became an attractive contender to host a major sports franchise. A group of investors that included singer Andy Williams, actor Tony Curtis, and composer Henry Mancini convinced the National Basketball Association (NBA) to grant the city a new franchise. The “pumpkin”—this time

FORWARD PAUL SILAS PALMED 11.7 REBOUNDS PER GAME IN THE 1969-70 SEASON.

in the form of a basketball—would be making a comeback in Phoenix, as the Suns hit the court in 1968.

Phoenix hired head coach Johnny "Red" Kerr—who had spent the previous two seasons getting another expansion team, the Chicago Bulls, up and running—to guide the Suns. However, Kerr was less successful with the Suns, who lost about four out of every five games in their inaugural season. The bright spots in the otherwise dim season were guards Gail Goodrich and Dick Van Arsdale, both of whom averaged more than 20 points per contest in the 1968–69 season.

Phoenix also boasted some solid rebounders, but the defense was lacking, and the Suns gave up more points than any other NBA team that season. Still, Arizona fans remained enthusiastic, filling the seats at Veterans Memorial Coliseum. "I didn't know how long we would last," said Coach Kerr. "I didn't know if people actually cared about basketball and would come out to the games. But they did, and they loved it."

The Suns would rise higher in the next three seasons, starting with a berth in the 1970 Western Division playoffs. This improvement

COURTSIDE STORIES

THE TOSS OF A COIN

A 16–66 record in the Suns' first season was difficult for some Phoenix fans to take, but by finishing with the worst record in the Western Conference, the team earned a chance to get the first pick in the 1969 NBA Draft. And in that draft, there was a huge prize looming: sensational University of California, Los Angeles (UCLA) center Lew Alcindor. Unfortunately, to get Alcindor (who would later change his name to Kareem Abdul-Jabbar), the Suns had to win a coin toss over the Milwaukee Bucks, a fellow expansion team that owned the Eastern Division's worst mark. The Bucks won the toss and took Alcindor (who would lead them to the 1971 NBA title), and the Suns settled for center Neal Walk. While Walk would have a respectable career, averaging 14.7 points per game in 5 seasons for Phoenix, the Suns would always wonder "What if?" "We had a group of young guys that would have fit perfectly with Alcindor," said Suns general manager Jerry Colangelo. "We would have been in a prime position to have a good long run if we had won that coin flip."

ALVAN ADAMS

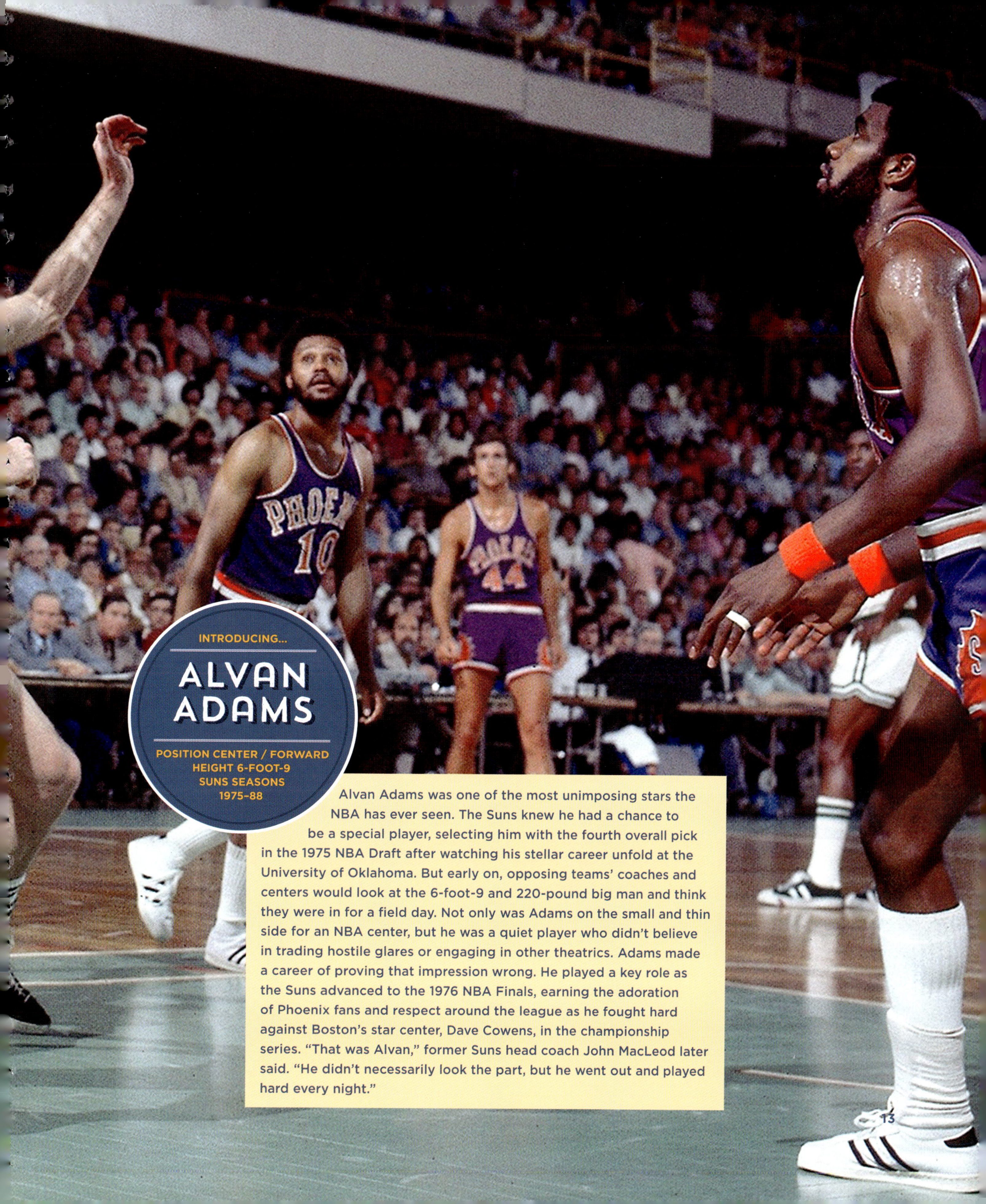

INTRODUCING...

ALVAN ADAMS

POSITION CENTER / FORWARD
HEIGHT 6-FOOT-9
SUNS SEASONS
1975–88

Alvan Adams was one of the most unimposing stars the NBA has ever seen. The Suns knew he had a chance to be a special player, selecting him with the fourth overall pick in the 1975 NBA Draft after watching his stellar career unfold at the University of Oklahoma. But early on, opposing teams' coaches and centers would look at the 6-foot-9 and 220-pound big man and think they were in for a field day. Not only was Adams on the small and thin side for an NBA center, but he was a quiet player who didn't believe in trading hostile glares or engaging in other theatrics. Adams made a career of proving that impression wrong. He played a key role as the Suns advanced to the 1976 NBA Finals, earning the adoration of Phoenix fans and respect around the league as he fought hard against Boston's star center, Dave Cowens, in the championship series. "That was Alvan," former Suns head coach John MacLeod later said. "He didn't necessarily look the part, but he went out and played hard every night."

> "HAWKINS IS A COMPLETE PLAYER. YOU HAVE TO LIKE HIM, BECAUSE HE PLAYS BOTH ENDS OF THE FLOOR. I'D HATE TO SEE HIM GET ANY BETTER. HE'S TOO GOOD NOW."
>
> — KNICKS COACH RED HOLZMAN ON CONNIE HAWKINS

was largely because of forward Connie Hawkins, who came aboard in 1969. Hawkins was an electrifying player who consistently swooped to the basket to unleash an array of crowd-pleasing dunks. Hawkins's game consisted of much more than just his skywalking act, though; he was also a great passer, using his long arms and huge hands to thread pinpoint passes to teammates cutting to the hoop.

Some fans criticized Hawkins as a showoff, and others said that the time he had spent away from the NBA (having been blackballed from the league for most of the '60s after his name came up in unsubstantiated gambling rumors) had diminished his game. Knicks coach Red Holzman, for one, dismissed such talk as ridiculous. "Hawkins is a complete player," he said. "You have to like him, because he plays both ends of the floor. I'd hate to see him get any better. He's too good now."

With Hawkins and fellow forward Paul Silas leading the way, the Suns went 48–34 in 1970–71. However, playing in the tough Midwest Division of the newly formed Western Conference, that record was not good enough for a postseason berth. The club's improvement continued the following year with a 49–33 record, but Phoenix again missed the playoffs, finishing behind the Milwaukee Bucks and Chicago Bulls.

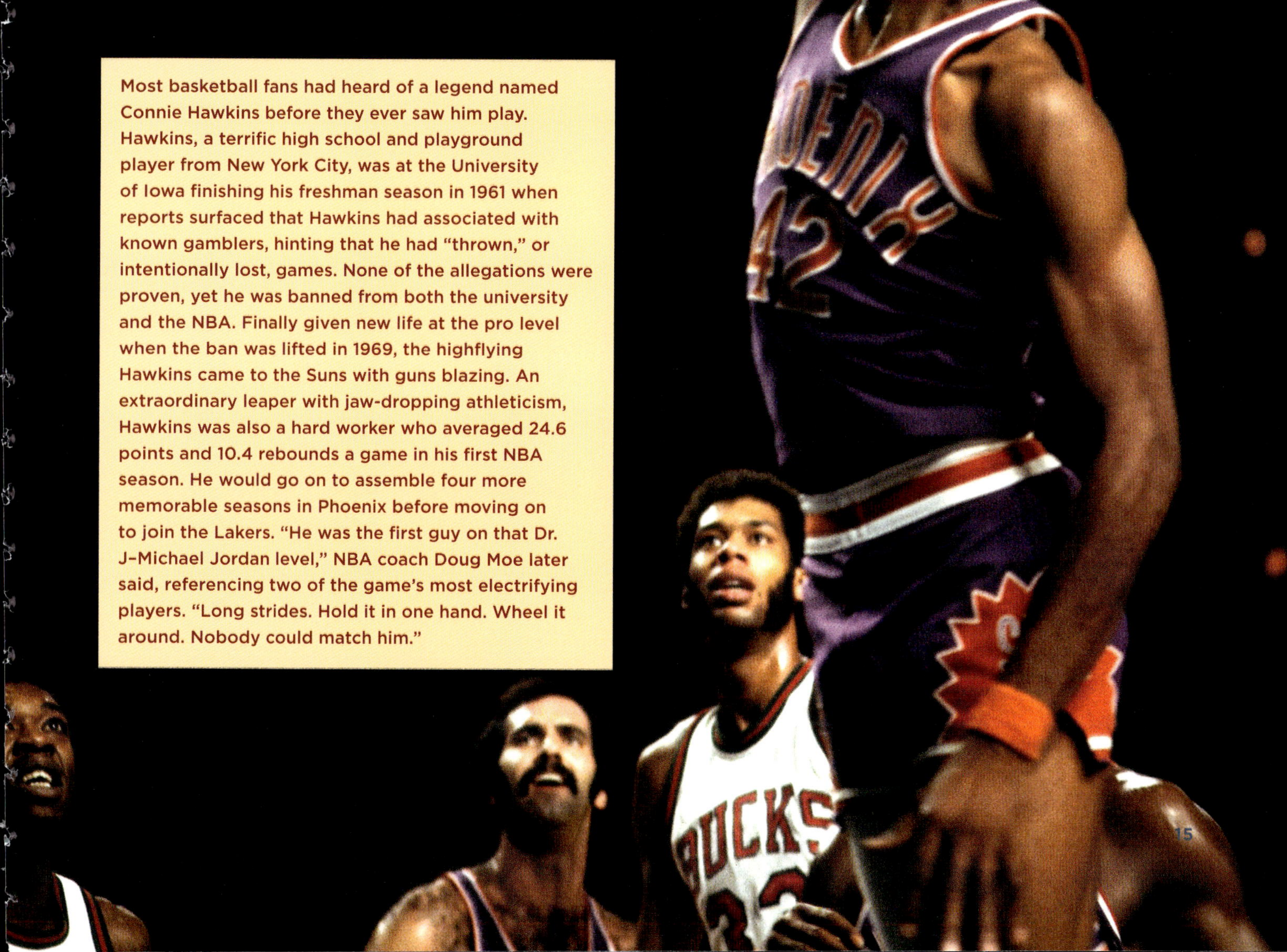

Most basketball fans had heard of a legend named Connie Hawkins before they ever saw him play. Hawkins, a terrific high school and playground player from New York City, was at the University of Iowa finishing his freshman season in 1961 when reports surfaced that Hawkins had associated with known gamblers, hinting that he had "thrown," or intentionally lost, games. None of the allegations were proven, yet he was banned from both the university and the NBA. Finally given new life at the pro level when the ban was lifted in 1969, the highflying Hawkins came to the Suns with guns blazing. An extraordinary leaper with jaw-dropping athleticism, Hawkins was also a hard worker who averaged 24.6 points and 10.4 rebounds a game in his first NBA season. He would go on to assemble four more memorable seasons in Phoenix before moving on to join the Lakers. "He was the first guy on that Dr. J–Michael Jordan level," NBA coach Doug Moe later said, referencing two of the game's most electrifying players. "Long strides. Hold it in one hand. Wheel it around. Nobody could match him."

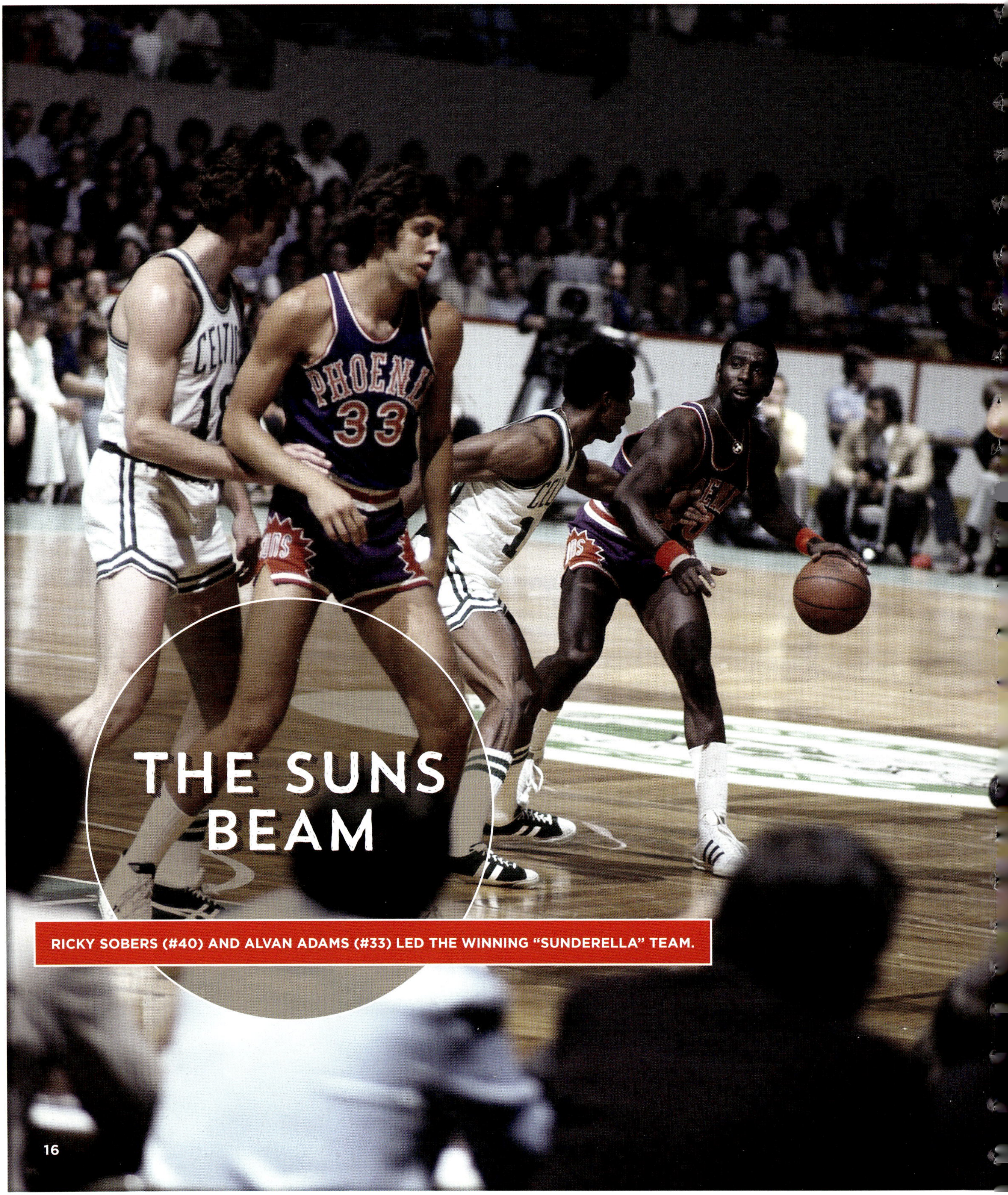

THE SUNS BEAM

RICKY SOBERS (#40) AND ALVAN ADAMS (#33) LED THE WINNING "SUNDERELLA" TEAM.

ALVAN ADAMS

The Suns had reason to be optimistic heading into 1972–73. They had improved their win-loss record every year, Hawkins had established himself as an NBA All-Star, and Van Arsdale continued to steady the team with his rock-solid play in the backcourt. Unfortunately, Phoenix regressed, falling back below .500, and general manager Jerry Colangelo made a coaching change, bringing in John MacLeod.

With a committed coach in place (MacLeod would remain as coach for 14 seasons), the Suns started looking to upgrade their talent level, too. They did just that in the 1975 NBA Draft, picking up center Alvan Adams and point guard Ricky Sobers in the first round. With this duo's youthful energy added to the mix, Phoenix bounced back with a 42–40 season and sneaked into the 1976 postseason.

Few fans expected the Suns to make much noise in

COURTSIDE STORIES

THE GREATEST GAME EVER?

The fifth game of the 1976 NBA Finals between the Suns and the Celtics has been called the greatest game ever played. Phoenix was a huge underdog in the series, but it had just won two home games to tie the series at two games apiece. In Boston, the confident young Suns pushed Game 5 into a third overtime period after making a brilliant strategic move. With time running out in the second overtime, Phoenix guard Paul Westphal called timeout, even though his team had none left. The Celtics were awarded a free throw (which they made) on a technical foul, but Phoenix was then able to inbound the ball at center court rather than from the far end. With the Suns trailing 112–110 with one second left, forward Curtis Perry inbounded the ball to forward Gar Heard, who caught it at the foul line, spun, and launched a high-arcing shot that hit nothing but net. Boston would win the game in the third overtime, but Heard's shot—and the Suns' overall effort—would go down in NBA lore.

PHOENIX
18
SUNS
PHOENIX
33

“IT’S A GAME THAT IS ALWAYS IN OUR MINDS, IT’S ONE OF THE MOST HISTORIC GAMES EVER, AND IT’S HARD NOT TO THINK ABOUT IT.”

– JERRY COLANGELO ON PHOENIX’S TRIPLE-OVERTIME LOSS TO BOSTON

the playoffs, as they had barely mustered a winning record. But Phoenix became the story of the 1976 NBA playoffs, beating the Seattle SuperSonics in round one, and then playing the defending NBA champion Golden State Warriors to a draw through six games of a best-of-seven series. Performing with a composure that belied their experience, Adams and the Suns went on the road in Game 7 and pulled off the impossible, downing the Warriors 94–86 to earn a spot in the NBA Finals.

Facing the upstart Suns in the Finals were the veteran Boston Celtics. The matchup pitted the fast-improving Adams against the Celtics’ best player, aggressive center Dave Cowens. Most fans expected Cowens, who could at times resemble a raging bull on the court, to dismantle the quiet and slender Adams. But a funny thing happened as the series unfolded. Adams showed no signs of being intimidated, battling Cowens gamely at both ends of the floor. The teams split the first four games. The fifth played out as one of the most exciting in NBA history.

Thanks to fine performances by Adams, Sobers, guard Paul Westphal, and forward Gar Heard, the Suns kept pace with the Celtics late into the fourth quarter … then into not one, but two overtime periods. With the screams of the Boston crowd ringing in his ears, Heard buried an incredible turnaround jumper at the end of the second overtime to tie the game at 112–112 and force yet a third extra session. Unfortunately for Suns fans, Boston then hung on for a 128–126 victory.

Two days later, Boston won Game 6 to take the championship. The Suns, despite the loss, had won league-wide respect, especially with their Game 5 heroics. “It’s a game that is always in our minds,” Colangelo said years later. “It’s one of the most historic games ever, and it’s hard not to think about it.”

INTRODUCING...

COTTON FITZSIMMONS

COACH
SUNS SEASONS
1970–72, 1988–92, 1995–96

Cotton Fitzsimmons, who served as the Suns' head coach for three different stints, was an affable and creative leader who inspired his charges to play with consistency and intensity. Fitzsimmons was also the Suns' director of player personnel during his second stint as head coach and was the man responsible for trading for point guard Kevin Johnson in 1988. The deal that saw the Suns swap star forward Larry Nance and another player to Cleveland for Johnson and two other players was widely criticized in Phoenix, but it changed the culture for a team that was losing both games and fan support. The Suns won 55 games in 1988–89, and Fitzsimmons was voted the NBA's Coach of the Year. Always quick with a quip, Fitzsimmons once explained his philosophy as a coach and personnel boss by saying, "You've got to be fired up with enthusiasm, or else we'll fire you with enthusiasm." For several years after hanging up his coaching whistle, Fitzsimmons remained a popular figure in Phoenix as a commentator for Suns television broadcasts.

KNOCKING AT THE DOOR

WALTER DAVIS BECAME THE SUNS' ALL-TIME SCORING LEADER WITH 15,666 POINTS.

PAUL WESTPHAL

Throughout the rest of the 1970s and into the mid-1980s, Phoenix continued to put strong lineups on the court. In 1978–79, the Suns—featuring Adams, Westphal, and guards Walter Davis and Don Buse—got off to a solid start. They then traded for New Orleans Jazz forward Leonard "Truck" Robinson at midseason. Robinson, as befitted his nickname, was a rugged, bruising player who established himself as a rebounding machine. The Suns finished the season 50–32, and then beat the Portland Trail Blazers and Kansas City Kings in the playoffs to advance to the Western Conference finals versus the SuperSonics. Needing just one more series victory to return to the grand stage of the NBA Finals, Phoenix came up short, losing four games to three.

After 4 more seasons in which Phoenix averaged more than 50 wins a year but suffered first- or second-round

PAUL WESTPHAL

COURTSIDE STORIES

PASSING FANCY

The Suns have employed different offensive schemes over the years, but they have been most successful when playing the game fast and passing the ball unselfishly. One of the most memorable such squads was the 1979–80 Suns, a team that finished with a 55–27 record. Featuring guards Paul Westphal and Walter Davis, forward Leonard "Truck" Robinson, and center Alvan Adams, the Suns were loaded with talented scorers. What made the team special, however, was its devotion to smart passing. Adams, Davis, Westphal, and point guard Don Buse each averaged four or more assists per game, making the Suns one of the most difficult teams in the league to defend. Head coach John MacLeod described the 1979–80 Suns as one of the best passing teams he was ever associated with. "You talk about passing and looking for the open man every play," MacLeod said. "I don't know that we ever had a team that did it any better than the Suns that year. It seemed like everyone got more out of making the good pass than they did hitting a shot."

playoff losses, the Suns struggled in 1983–84. They went a mere 41–41 but—as had been the case in 1976—slipped into the playoffs and found their groove. With Davis providing much of the team's backcourt scoring (Westphal was sidelined by injury), and with highflying forward Larry Nance spearheading Phoenix's low-post efforts, the Suns got by Portland and the Utah Jazz in the first two rounds of the playoffs, only to fall to the Los Angeles Lakers in the conference finals.

In 1985–86, the Suns missed the playoffs for the first time in nine years. As they looked at their roster, Colangelo and Phoenix player personnel director Cotton Fitzsimmons concluded that the Suns needed more youth. And so, in 1988, they swapped experience for speed and enthusiasm by trading Nance and forward Mike Sanders to the Cleveland Cavaliers for super-quick rookie point guard Kevin Johnson, center Mark West, and forward Ty Corbin. Nance had been an All-Star in Phoenix,

LEAPIN' LARRY NANCE FLEW OVER EVEN LEGENDARY KAREEM ABDUL-JABAAR (#33).

COURTSIDE STORIES

THE SUNS GORILLA

The Phoenix Suns Gorilla is arguably the most famous mascot in all of North American sports. The furry mascot started his act with what was supposed to be a one-time-only halftime routine in a 1980 game. The fans in Phoenix's Veterans Memorial Coliseum roared louder for the Gorilla than they did for their team, and he was invited back regularly before becoming a standard part of the franchise's pregame and halftime routine. From 1988 to 2006, the man inside the costume was Bob Woolf, a former private investigator from Boston. Woolf worked out constantly in order to be able to complete his stunts, which included leaping off a trampoline through a flaming ring of fire for a slam dunk. "In this job," Woolf said, "you never know what is going to come next. We try to give the fans just what they want—and a little more." Over the years, the Gorilla has become something of a cultural icon, even appearing in the popular *NBA Jam* video game in the 1990s. In 2005, he became a charter member of the Mascot Hall of Fame.

SUNS
ONE

"WE KNEW WE WERE SO CLOSE, BUT AT THE SAME TIME, THERE WAS SOMETHING MORE THAT WE NEEDED. WE JUST NEEDED TO GET A LITTLE STRONGER ... AND FIND THAT TOUGHNESS WE NEEDED."

— KEVIN JOHNSON ON THE WESTERN CONFERENCE FINALS

but the Suns rightly saw Johnson as one of the NBA's up-and-coming stars. West, the other pivotal part of the trade, was coming into his own as a fearsome rebounder and shot blocker.

Johnson, known to fans as "KJ," was a rarity: he was a point guard who could use his quickness to get open shots and score bunches of points, and one who also rarely turned the ball over and energized his teammates with his unselfish passing. "It didn't take long to know that he was special," Colangelo later said. "We knew he was a good player when we made the move, and he turned out to be better than we anticipated."

The Suns built their lineup and game plan around KJ's speed, surrounding him with teammates such as forward Tom Chambers, swingman Dan Majerle, and guards Eddie Johnson and Jeff Hornacek, all of whom could run and shoot. In 1988–89, Phoenix emerged as one of the most explosive teams in the league, finishing 55–27 and marching into the playoffs with momentum. It rolled over the Denver Nuggets in three straight games before taking apart the Warriors in a round-two rout. There was nothing but confidence in the Suns' locker room as they prepared to engage the mighty Lakers in the Western Conference finals. But Los Angeles—the NBA's premier dynasty of the '80s—was still too powerful, topping Phoenix in four close games.

A second straight loss in the Western Conference finals in 1990, this time to Portland, convinced Suns management that another big move was in order. "We knew we were so close, but at the same time, there was something more that we needed," Kevin Johnson later said. "We just needed to get a little stronger ... and find that toughness we needed."

INTRODUCING...

KEVIN JOHNSON

POSITION GUARD
HEIGHT 6-FOOT-1
SUNS SEASONS
1988–98, 1999–2000

Kevin Johnson was just a rookie with potential when the Suns traded for him during the 1987–88 season. Phoenix personnel director Cotton Fitzsimmons believed his plodding club needed a shot in the arm, and Johnson turned out to be the perfect medicine, transforming the Suns into a high-octane, highly entertaining team. An excellent ball handler and deft passer, Johnson could shoot and pass with equal aplomb, and he asserted leadership even as one of the team's youngest players. Throughout his 12 seasons in Phoenix, Johnson averaged 18.7 points and 9.5 assists per game. As of 2014, he was 1 of only 3 players in NBA history to have averaged at least 20 points and 10 assists in 3 consecutive seasons. The humble Johnson credited Fitzsimmons (who became head coach in 1988) with giving him the confidence he needed to become an NBA superstar. "He told me we were going as far as I could take us," Johnson said. "That meant everything to me." After his basketball career ended, Johnson decided to move into politics and was elected the mayor of Sacramento, California, in 2008 and re-elected in 2012.

A CHANGE OF ATTITUDE

THE ARRIVAL OF ALL-STAR CHARLES BARKLEY MARKED A NEW ERA IN SUNS BASKETBALL.

STEVE NASH

By the start of the 1990s, the "run-and-gun" Suns had gone as far as KJ alone could take them. The point guard remained a speedy dynamo, but while the Suns continued to win a lot of games, they were not a legitimate title contender. In 1992, they made headlines with a transaction intended to change that, trading Hornacek, forward Tim Perry, and center Andrew Lang to the Philadelphia 76ers for All-Star forward Charles Barkley.

Barkley was a fearless, rough-and-tumble player who combined well-balanced skills with great physical strength. Known as both "The Round Mound of Rebound" and "Sir Charles," he had been the main man in Philadelphia for years, but the 76ers were on a downhill slide. When Barkley asked to be traded, he was pleased to find himself headed to the Valley of the Sun.

STEVE NASH

COURTSIDE STORIES

THE TURNAROUND

Things couldn't have seemed much worse for the Suns than they did in 2003–04, when Phoenix went 29–53. The team was young and rebuilding, but even the most ardent Suns supporter couldn't foresee what was about to happen in 2004–05. The Suns had just named Mike D'Antoni their new coach, and before the season, they added point guard Steve Nash and athletic swingman Quentin Richardson. Buoyed by D'Antoni's fast-paced game plan and Nash's confident on-court leadership, the Suns surged to an unbelievable 62–20 record, easily setting a franchise record with a 33-win improvement in the span of 1 year. As Nash slung the ball to such talented teammates as forwards Shawn Marion and Amar'e Stoudemire, Phoenix games became some of the hottest tickets in the NBA. The Suns streaked all the way to the Western Conference finals, and even though they were beaten in five games by the eventual NBA champion Spurs, Phoenix was a team reborn. "We feel like we bring it every night," said Nash, who was named NBA MVP, "and we demand the best of ourselves."

"HE'D CARRIED THIS TEAM SO MANY TIMES, AND THAT GAME HE CAME OUT AND CARRIED US."

– DAN MAJERLE ON CHARLES BARKLEY

The chemistry between KJ, Barkley, Majerle, and new head coach Paul Westphal was tremendous, and the 1992–93 Suns went a sensational 62–20 to claim the top seed in the Western Conference playoffs. Their record was best in the league, which meant that if they could reach the NBA Finals, they would have the home-court advantage over their opponent—a team everyone believed would be superstar guard Michael Jordan's Chicago Bulls.

Dreams of the Finals nearly died in the first round, though, as the Suns lost the first two games at home to the Lakers. Coach Westphal put pressure on his team by guaranteeing they would go to Los Angeles and win two games. The Suns did just that, and then they beat the Lakers in the decisive Game 5 at Phoenix's America West Arena.

The next round was no easier, but Phoenix ultimately beat the San Antonio Spurs in six games to earn a spot in the conference finals against Seattle. The Suns and SuperSonics split the first six games. Then, with Game 7 in Phoenix and a trip to the Finals on the line, the Suns stepped up their efforts and notched a 123–110 win. Barkley, in particular, was outstanding. The star forward declared before the game that he would score 40 points and get 20 rebounds, and he made good on his promise by scoring 44 points and grabbing 24 boards. His teammates were not surprised. "I knew he could," Majerle said. "He'd done it so many times. He'd carried this team so many times, and that game he came out and carried us."

Next up in the Finals were indeed the Bulls, and Barkley and Jordan took center stage. It appeared the series would be a rout after the Bulls won the first two games in Phoenix, but thanks to the three-headed attack of Barkley, Majerle, and Johnson, the Suns stayed alive by winning two of three games in Chicago. After claiming a 108–98 victory in Game 5, the Suns returned home with momentum. It was not to be, though. Jordan scored 33 points in Game 6 and threw a perfect pass to wide-open Bulls guard John Paxson, who hit the series-winning shot in a 99–98 Chicago win.

The Finals loss to the Bulls, though bitter, did not send the Suns into a depression. They added forward A. C. Green and center Joe Kleine and remained one of the strongest teams in the league in each of the next two seasons. However, both of those years ended with second-round playoff defeats to the eventual

INTRODUCING...

AMAR'E STOUDEMIRE

POSITION FORWARD
HEIGHT 6-FOOT-10
SUNS SEASONS
2002–10

Many basketball observers thought Amar'e Stoudemire made a huge mistake when he decided to enter the 2002 NBA Draft directly out of his Orlando, Florida, high school instead of going to the University of Memphis. Over the years, quite a few high-school stars had bypassed playing college basketball to go to the NBA, and most had failed. As Stoudemire quickly proved, he would not be one of them. The broad-shouldered forward was an energetic force who played fearlessly against the NBA's best big men. In his first season, Stoudemire averaged 13.5 points and 8.8 rebounds per game and was named NBA Rookie of the Year. After that, he emerged as a legitimate star by averaging 20 or more points per game in 6 of the next 7 seasons. Besides his explosive vertical leap and superb instincts, self-confidence was one of Stoudemire's greatest attributes. "Since the age of eight, I knew I would make it to the NBA," he said. "When I played ball, I was always a little bit better, a little taller, a little faster, and that kept my confidence going."

NBA champion Houston Rockets. The Suns took leads in both of those series, only to see Houston bounce back and claim the title in seven games.

Realizing that their losses to Houston were due largely to defensive weaknesses, the Suns made a move to exchange offense for defense, trading Majerle to Cleveland for center John "Hot Rod" Williams. The move did not pay off, as the 1995–96 Suns went 41–41 and then cleaned house, trading Barkley to the Rockets for forwards Mark Bryant, Chucky Brown, and Robert Horry.

Phoenix refused to fade, returning to the playoffs in 1997 and then posting a strong 56–26 record the following season. The 1997–98 Suns demonstrated a defensive tenacity that had long been lacking, going 45–9 when holding opponents to 100 points or fewer. However, the joy of the regular season was again overshadowed by postseason disappointment as the Spurs and star center David Robinson bounced the Suns in the first round.

That same pattern played out the next three seasons. After Johnson retired in 1998 (he would return briefly in 1999–2000), point guards Jason Kidd and, later, Stephon Marbury, put forth some exciting offensive showings, and two new coaches—former NBA guards Danny Ainge and Scott Skiles—tried their hand at leading the team. None of these new players nor coaches, though, could return the Suns to contender status.

DESPITE A BACKCOURT LED BY JASON KIDD, THE TEAM WAS REPEATEDLY SHUT OUT OF THE FINALS.

STEPHON MARBURY HAD LETHAL ON-COURT INSTINCTS AND A KNACK FOR DRIVING TO THE HOOP.

RUN-AND-GUN RISES AGAIN

SIGNING WITH PHOENIX REVIVED VETERAN FORWARD GRANT HILL'S PLAYING CAREER.

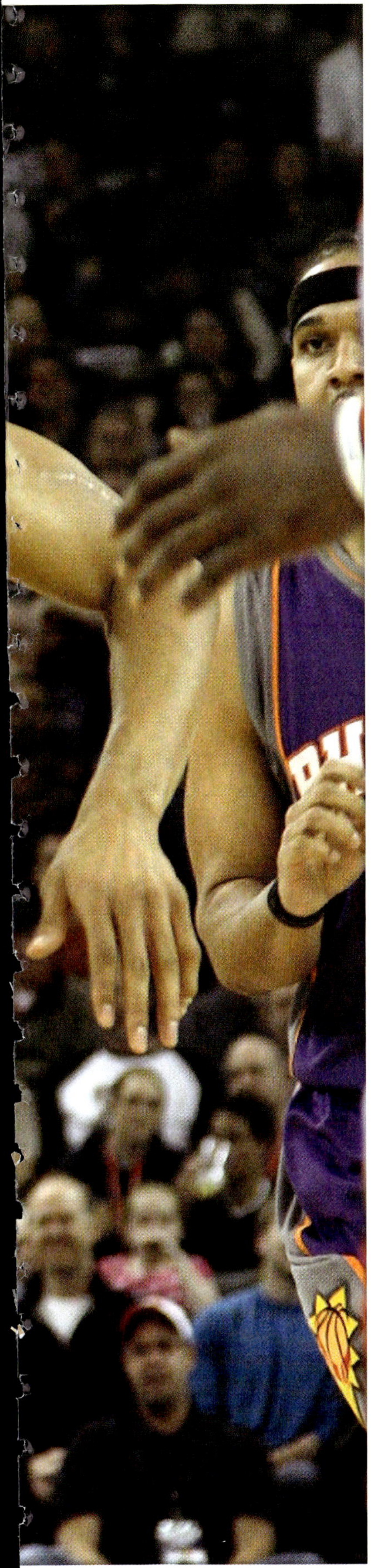

SHAQUILLE O'NEAL

In the midst of the 2001–02 season, the Suns were a .500 team under Skiles. In hopes of shaking the squad from mediocrity, Phoenix made a coaching change, bringing in Frank Johnson. The Suns' performance actually declined the remainder of the year, finishing 36–46, but Johnson laid the groundwork for a faster style of play.

This theoretical change got a practical boost when Phoenix drafted strapping forward/center Amar'e Stoudemire to run the floor with Marbury and all-purpose forward Shawn "The Matrix" Marion. Scoring production increased in 2002–03, putting the young Suns back in the postseason. But as a leaky defense hampered Phoenix the following year, Marbury was dealt away and new head coach Mike D'Antoni took the bench.

The Suns tweaked their approach going into the 2004–05 season. D'Antoni wanted an up-tempo but controlled

SEVEN-FOOT-1 CENTER SHAQUILLE O'NEAL TIPPED THE BALL IN PHOENIX'S FAVOR IN THE LATE 2000s.

style, and there was no one better to rein in such an offense than point guard Steve Nash. The former Dallas Mavericks star was a remarkable shooter, but even more appealing was his ball control and ability to spread the ball around to create easy scoring opportunities for teammates. "It was no secret as to how good Steve was before he got here," said D'Antoni. "But once you see him operate day after day, it was a pretty awesome experience."

Nash led the league in assists in both 2004–05 and 2005–06 while shooting better than 50 percent from the field and 43 percent from beyond the arc. More importantly, he made the Suns a legitimate contender again, leading the club to 62 and 54 wins respectively during those two seasons. For his efforts, Nash won the NBA Most Valuable Player (MVP) award in both 2005 and 2006. Regular-season success finally translated to some postseason victories as well, as Phoenix reached the Western Conference finals after each of Nash's MVP seasons.

The Suns continued to light up NBA scoreboards in 2006–07, averaging 110 points a game, posting a 61–21 record, and winning their third straight Pacific Division title. The core of Nash, Stoudemire, and Marion was as good as ever, and, much to the dismay of opponents, young guard Leandro Barbosa emerged as a deadly shooter. Once again, though, the

INTRODUCING...

STEVE NASH

POSITION GUARD
HEIGHT 6-FOOT-3
SUNS SEASONS 1996–98, 2004–12

As Steve Nash claimed two NBA MVP awards while orchestrating the Suns' sensational fast-break offense, he made everything look effortless. In reality, though, his polished performances were the result of countless hours spent in the gym perfecting his craft. When the Suns made the point guard their first choice in the 1996 NBA Draft, fans reacted with boos. "I don't look like I'm going to be a tremendous basketball player on appearance," Nash said at the time. "I probably would've booed myself too, but I'm going to be a really good player. I have a lot of faith in myself, and hopefully they'll enjoy watching me play." Nash played two unremarkable seasons for the Suns before they traded him to Dallas in 1998. Through hard work, he became one of the best point guards in the league there, and the Suns brought him back as a free agent in 2004. He immediately transformed Phoenix into a Western Conference force with his rare court vision and passing flair. In 2012, Nash was traded to the Los Angeles Lakers.

APS
SIXERS
42
LifeLock
FULTON HOMES

AFTER ARRIVING IN ARIZONA IN 2008, FORWARD JARED DUDLEY PROVED HIS DURABILITY.

COURTSIDE STORIES

BRAWL IN THE DESERT

When the Phoenix Suns hosted the New York Knicks on March 24, 1993, each team held the top record in its respective conference. The game was considered a pre-playoff glimpse of who was truly the NBA's best team. The teams also shared a reputation for tenacious play and fiery emotions. As the first half of the game wound down, both teams took exception to the physical play of their opponents and began applauding referee calls against their foes. And after the Suns' Kevin Johnson plowed through a Doc Rivers screen with a neck-high forearm, Rivers ran down Johnson. The guards exchanged punches, and benches cleared. Just as things seemed to be calming down, Knicks guard Greg Anthony sucker-punched a restrained Johnson, reigniting the melee. When the dust settled, six players, including Johnson, Rivers, and Anthony were ejected. "I've never seen anything like it in all my 27 years in the league," said Suns president Jerry Colangelo. "It got a little scary there for a minute." Phoenix was victorious by night's end, but neither club would go on to the NBA title, as the Chicago Bulls defeated both teams.

Suns failed to rise in the playoffs, losing in the second round.

In the midst of a solid 2007–08, a bold trade sent Marion to the Miami Heat for center Shaquille O'Neal. O'Neal—once the most dominant player in the league—was still a force in the post, grabbing 10.6 rebounds per game and hitting 61 percent of his shots, but his 35-year-old, 300-plus pound body did not mesh with the Suns' fast-paced offense. Phoenix lost in the first round of the 2008 playoffs and missed the 2009 postseason entirely.

After O'Neal was traded to Cleveland, Nash and Stoudemire were left to lead the club under new coach Alvin Gentry. "Obviously if we're a contender again, that's great—that's where everyone wants to be," Nash said. "But I think right now I'd be happy to be part of a really positive, optimistic atmosphere, be a part of a team that is really on the same page, plays together, plays hard every night, and makes the season exciting for one another and for the fans." The 2009–10 Suns proved to be both a cohesive unit and a playoffs contender, going 54–28 and surging all the way to the conference finals before falling to the Lakers.

The run-and-gun Suns seemed to hit another roadblock after the season, though. Unable to afford Stoudemire, Phoenix had to deal him to the Knicks. Barbosa was also sent packing. Phoenix declined in each of the next two seasons, missing the playoffs both years.

Rebuilding was clearly in order, and because keeping an aging point guard on board made little sense, Phoenix bid farewell to Nash. The 2012–13 Suns limped to just 25 wins—the fewest since the club's inaugural season. But a few young building blocks offered hope for the future. Point guard Goran Dragic posted career highs in points, assists, and steals; center Marcin "The Polish Hammer" Gortat exhibited toughness inside; and forward Jared Dudley provided a deft shooting touch. Players felt they were finally starting to gel near the season's end. "Everybody was involved, everybody was making shots," Dragic said after a late-season victory. "On defense, we were talking, and we played well. If we would play like this earlier, for sure we would be close to the playoffs."

The Suns continued tinkering with their roster before the 2013–14 season, trading Dudley and Gortat and adding players such as sweet-shooting point guard Eric Bledsoe and 6-foot-11 swingman Miles Plumlee. By February, Phoenix had surpassed the previous season's total wins with 30 victories to defy expectations. Although it ended the season with a 48–34 record, that wasn't enough to catapult the team into the glow of the playoffs.

Pumpkinville may be a name that still applies to Phoenix, but for the past half century, it's been the leather pumpkin that has been a focal point of the city. While championship glory has eluded them, the Suns have almost always been tough competitors with a history of burning speedsters, blistering passers, and net-scorching shooters. Fans who call the desert oasis home have little doubt that an NBA title will be diverted to Phoenix any year now.

PHOENIX
11
SUNS

GORAN DRAGIC'S PRECISION PASSES OFTEN CREATED KEY SCORING OPPORTUNITIES.

INDEX